Little Crooked House

For Pola and JoJo. M.W.
For Mum and Dad. J.B.

Published in 2006 by Simply Read Books
www.simplyreadbooks.com

First published in Australia by ABC Books
for the Australian Broadcasting Corporation

Cataloguing in Publication Data

Wild, Margaret, 1948-

The little crooked house / Margaret Wild ; illustrated
by Jonathan Bentley.

ISBN-10: 1-894965-59-0
ISBN-13: 978-1-894965-59-0

I. Bentley, Jonathan II. Title.

PZ7.W64Li 2006 j823'.914 C2006-900134-0

Edited by Margaret Hamilton
The illustrations were created with watercolors
Color reproduction by Graphic Print Group, Adelaide
Printed and bound in Malaysia by Tien Wah Press

10 9 8 7 6 5 4 3 2 1

The Little Crooked House

Written by Margaret Wild

Illustrated by Jonathan Bentley

Simply Read Books

Once, there was a crooked man,
and he walked a crooked mile.

He found a crooked sixpence
beside a crooked stile.

He bought a crooked cat,
which found a crooked mouse.

And they all lived together
in a little crooked house.

But the little crooked house had

been built right on the edge of a railway track.

Every day when the train thundered past,
the little crooked house shook —

shucka-shucka, shucka-shucka, shucka-shucka!

One morning when the train came roaring
down the track as usual, the crooked man said
to the cat and the mouse and the house,

"One of these days we'll be shaken to bits.

We have to move."

So with a creak and a groan,
the little crooked house heaved
itself up, and took a step.

One step,

two steps,

three steps, four.

Then it ran.

"Come back, come back, little crooked house!"
called the train.

But the little crooked house ran
over the hill and far away.

And the crooked man and the crooked cat
and the crooked mouse held on tight and sang,

"Yippee-yi-yay!"

The little crooked house ran
without stopping until it came to a desert.

The crooked man and the crooked cat went
walking in the cool of the night, and the
crooked mouse played with the desert mice,
popping in and out of their burrows.

But every day, all day, hot winds blew —

whoooo-whoooo, whoooo-whooo

hoooo-whoooo!

Sand piled up around the little crooked house, and the crooked man said to the cat and the mouse and the house, "One of these days we'll be buried in sand. We have to move."

So with a creak and a groan, the little crooked
house heaved itself up, and took a step.

One step,

two steps,

three steps, four.

Then it ran.

"Come back, come back, little crooked house!"
called the desert wind.

But the little crooked house
ran over the sand dunes and far away.

And the crooked man and the crooked cat
and the crooked mouse held on tight and sang,
"Yippee-yi-yay!"

The little crooked house ran without
stopping until it came to a wide, wide river.

The crooked man and the crooked cat went fishing.
And the crooked mouse played hide-and-seek
with the river mice.

But one day, it rained and rained and rained.

The river rose up and flowed swiftly —

"Swish-swoosh, swish-swoosh, swish-swoosh!"

As water swirled around the house, the crooked man
said to the cat and the mouse and the house,
"One of these days the river will wash us away.
We have to move."

So with a creak and a groan, the little crooked
house heaved itself up and took a step.

One step,

two steps,

three steps, four.

Then it ran.

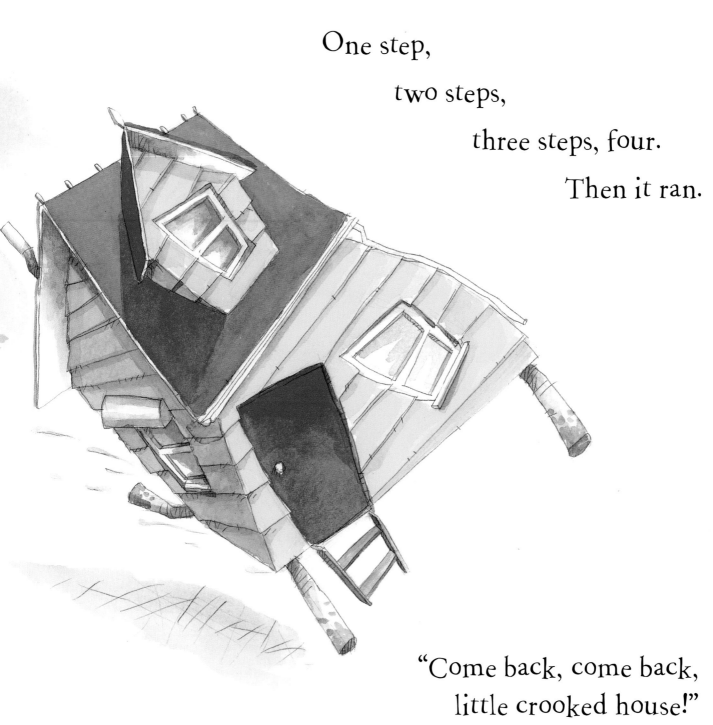

"Come back, come back,
little crooked house!"
called the wide, wide river.

But the little crooked house ran through the
muddy waters and far away.

And the crooked man and the crooked cat
and the crooked mouse held on tight and sang,

"Yippee-yi-yay!"

The little crooked house ran without stopping,
until it came to a city. It looked this way and that.

And then it sat itself down
between two big houses.

The crooked man put his chair out the front,
the crooked cat lazed on the windowsill,
and the crooked mouse played tag with
the mice from the big houses.

One summer evening, the crooked man said, "Here we will not
be shaken to bits, or buried in sand, or washed away by the river.
Here we are safe, and here we will stay for ever and ever."

So with a creak and a groan,
the little crooked house
anchored itself to the ground.

And the crooked man and the crooked cat and the crooked mouse danced from room to room, singing,

"Yippee-yi-yay!"

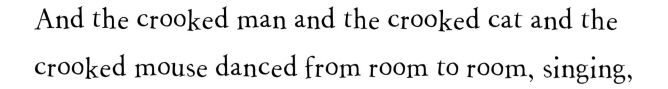